Fresh Brewed Tales from the Coffee Bar

(Eleven One-Act Plays)

by

Henry Meyerson

A Samuel French Acting Edition

SAMUEL FRENCH

FOUNDED 1830

NEW YORK HOLLYWOOD LONDON TORONTO

SAMUELFRENCH.COM

ISBN 978-0-573-66039-9   Printed in U.S.A.   #8231

MUSIC USE NOTE

Licensees are solely responsible for obtaining formal written permission from copyright owners to use copyrighted music in the performance of this play and are strongly cautioned to do so. If no such permission is obtained by the licensee, then the licensee must use only original music that the licensee owns and controls. Licensees are solely responsible and liable for all music clearances and shall indemnify the copyright owners of the play and their licensing agent, Samuel French, Inc., against any costs, expenses, losses and liabilities arising from the use of music by licensees.

IMPORTANT BILLING AND CREDIT REQUIREMENTS

All producers of *FRESH BREWED: TALES FROM THE COFFEE BAR* must give credit to the Author of the Play in all programs distributed in connection with performances of the Play, and in all instances in which the title of the Play appears for the purposes of advertising, publicizing or otherwise exploiting the Play and/or a production. The name of the Author *must* appear on a separate line on which no other name appears, immediately following the title and *must* appear in size of type not less than fifty percent of the size of the title type.

In addition the following credit *must* be given in all programs and publicity information distributed in association with this piece:

Several **FRESH BREWED** plays have been appropriated from my one-act collection, *JAVA JIVE*. For their help in the development and productions of *JAVA JIVE*, I'd like to thank Michael Bradford, Producer, James Alexander Bond, Director, and original cast members Todd Allen Durkin, Karen Leeds, Tanya Moberly, John Sama, and Gregg Weiner. Other plays in this collection owe their development to New Jersey Dramatists, Peter Ernst and Kerri Kochanski, Co-Artistic Directors, and Times Square Playwrights, Tom Thornton, Artistic Director. And, as always, I owe my personal development to Ronnie's love and support.

Note to Directors

If all of the plays are performed in one evening, there should be no black outs between plays. Over the years, I've discovered when the lights come up after a black out, there are less people in the audience. Simply changing the composition of the cast can signal the audience of movement between plays while also keeping the audience in their seats. On the hand, each play is written so it can be performed as a stand-alone work.

If done as a unit, I suggest the following order. At the least, I would recommend opening with NO PRUNE, and closing with I FELL SWELL. The plays and casting are as follows:

Cast of 2m, 2f. Casting works best if all are approximately the same age, late twenties and thirties.

No Prune - 1m, 1f
Morning Coffee – 2m, 1f
Hierarchy – 2m
Him – 2f
Alice – 1f
This Has Been Some Day – 2m, 2f
Class – 1m, 1f
Hopeful Alice – 1m, 1f
George And Martha – 1m, 1f
Happy Birthday – 2m
I Feel Swell - 2m, 2f

NO PRUNE

NO PRUNE premiered at the 1998 Samuel French Short Play Festival, New York, directed by Mildred Purdy. Subsequent performances were at Avery Point Playhouse, 1999 and The Producers Club, 2000, both directed by James Alexander Bond, at Midtown International Theatre Festival, 2000, directed by Charles Armesto, First Stage, LA, 2002, directed by Bill Becker, and at Sticky, Sheffield, UK, directed by Lisa Charles.

CAST

ALLEN

CARMEN

(AT LIGHTS: **ALLEN** *sitting at a table as if in a cata-tonic state. A cup of coffee and a Danish are in front of him, untouched. He seems lost in reverie. After pos-sibly a minute of* **ALLEN** *staring blankly at the Danish, he reaches for it just as we hear a loud, strident, female VOICE, YELLING off stage.*

CARMEN (O.S.) SAME TO YOU TO, PAL. *(beat)* SO GIVE ME A TICKET. I'LL PARK WHERE EVER THE HELL I WANT.

(After a brief pause, **CARMEN** *enters in a whirlwind.* **ALLEN** *looks on as if he were suddenly confronted by a threat to life and limb.* **CARMEN** *seems in a fluster, her hair a tangle over her shoulders and face. She wears mini-skirt, boots, and is not adverse to fish-net stockings. Her blouse may have been tucked in her skirt at the start of the day, but by now it's on its own.)*

CARMEN (CONT'D) Anybody got any change? I need a dollar worth of change. *(staring directly into Allen's face)* Any-body got change? The cop is giving me a ticket unless I pay the meter.

ALLEN. *(timidly)* Wha..? Oh...

*(*ALLEN** *hands her some silver which she takes, but then neglects to give him his dollar.* **CARMEN** *rushes off-stage.* **ALLEN** *takes the moment to reorganize himself.* **CARMEN** *re-enters.)*

CARMEN. Ass-hole.

ALLEN. Did he give you a tick..?

(Ignoring him, **CARMEN** *produces a cell phone and makes a call.)*

CARMEN. Hello, Dave, it's me. *(beat)* What difference does it make where I am? *(beat)* Wait a second, Dave, I never said that. *(beat)* Well, you misunderstood. *(beat)* Look, Dave, I don't give a shit what you think I said, I never said that. Anyway, I had the decency to call, and this is the shit I get. *(beat)* Yeah, well, up yours, too, shithead.

(CARMEN angrily SLAMS the cell phone shut, looks feverishly around the restaurant, then sits in the chair next to ALLEN. She's breathing hard. ALLEN senses he is in the presence of lunacy.)

ALLEN. Tough call.

CARMEN. That putz. He had the nerve to think I was going move in with him. In Brooklyn, yet. Can you imagine? What a jerk. I sleep with him a couple of times and he wants to put a leash on me. Fuck him.

ALLEN. Right, fuck him. Did you say what he thought you said?

CARMEN. Of course, but I could never admit that. Then he would really have a case against me. What are you eating?

(ALLEN looks increasingly uncomfortable.)

ALLEN. It's a Dan...

(CARMEN sticks a finger into the cherry center of the Danish and then loudly sucks on her finger.)

CARMEN. Mmmm. Good. Cherry. I like cherry. Better than prune, ya know? You don't eat prune, do ya?

ALLEN. *(timidly)* Nah.

CARMEN. What?

ALLEN. I don't eat prune.

CARMEN. Only old constipated people eat prunes. Ugh. Right?

ALLEN. *(obviously changing the subject)* You working around here?

CARMEN. Yeah, well, not really. I mean I was. I got fired yesterday. I was doing the dining room, waitressing, you know, at the Concordia hotel. The big place up the street. Anyway, some slob who thought he was a big deal because he had a suite at the hotel started putting his hands on me so I belted him. They fired me.

ALLEN. Good for you.

CARMEN. Nah, not really. He'd been doing the same thing all week. I was a little wired from all the pills I was taking so I kinda lost control. I didn't mind his hands. I mean, I'd been banging the guy, so what the hell does a little feel mean, you know?

ALLEN. Oh, sure.

CARMEN. Thinks he owns me.

ALLEN. Did you like the guy?

CARMEN. What difference does that make? I'm telling you, if it wasn't for the pills I'd still be working there and banging the guy.

ALLEN. *(obviously uncomfortable)* How'd you like working there ?

CARMEN. It was a strange place. Like the first week I got here. I didn't have a job so I had to stay in a hotel for a few days. Anyway, the first morning I went to the coffee shop for breakfast. I ordered grapefruit juice. I always have grapefruit juice. So I'm sitting there in a fog like I always am in the morning just trying to remember who I am and where the fuck I am and I'm reading the morning paper and I look down and I'm holding the juice glass and its empty.

(now more slowly, warily)

But the thing is, I don't remember drinking the juice. So now I'm really uneasy, because I got this empty juice glass in my hand, but I don't know if I drank it or spilled it or what, you know? So I call the waiter over and ask him if he remembered me drinking the juice and he said he wasn't watching that close. So I asked him if he remembered pouring the juice and he smiled and said he did.

(more frantically)

So I'm feeling relieved now, because now I know that

I had juice in the glass and now that it's empty I must have drunk it.

(warily, again, suspicious)

But then I notice the waiter kind of look at me out of the corner of his eye and smirk a little. I'm sure it was a smirk, so now I'm thinking that he just said he poured the juice, but he really didn't. I mean, why else would he smirk? So now I don't know what to think. I mean, how can I prove he did or he didn't? There was no evidence. I either drank it, or he never poured it. *(beat)* What do you think?

ALLEN. About what?

CARMEN. About whether or not the waiter really poured the juice. What do you think?

ALLEN. Why would the waiter lie?

CARMEN. That's a stupid question. By not pouring the juice and charging me they make more money and the waiter gets a bigger tip and they get to keep the juice.

ALLEN. Ah, so this is a great juice scam, is that it?

CARMEN. Exactly.

(**ALLEN** *stands, takes two dollars from his wallet and places is on the table.*)

ALLEN. Well, I think my little space travel is about over.

CARMEN. Oh, no, I've done it again. I always do something like this. I've frightened you.

ALLEN. No, no, I'll be all right.

CARMEN. No, really, I came on too strong. Right? Admit it.

ALLEN. No, no, it was fine.

CARMEN. I SAID ADMIT IT.

ALLEN. I...I... okay, well, maybe just a tad stronger than I can handle, actually.

CARMEN. I know, I know. I try. I say to myself, Carmen, that's my name, Carmen...

ALLEN. Oh, hi, I'm Allen.

CARMEN. *(ignoring him)* ...you've got to get control of your life. You just can't be running around cursing cops, dropping pills, snorting, smoking and whatever, fucking anything with a dick or without. You got to behave yourself.

ALLEN. Does it work?

CARMEN. Now that's another stupid question. Didn't you just hear me, see me in action, see me rip off your dollar?

ALLEN. I did.

CARMEN. Don't you think that's messed up?

ALLEN. I do.

CARMEN. Do you have any questions?

ALLEN. No, no I don't.

CARMEN. You don't want to know how come I'm so fucked up, what about my past contributed to this mess that I am, what my parents think about their pretty little daughter, the apple of their eye, the girl they had their hopes on, the girl they bet all their hard earned money on when they packed her off to college and good riddance? Don't you want to know about the shrinks, the flock of fucking Freudian frauds that bled me and my family for five years until I fled on foot over flooded farmland and fences to find freedom in this fucking forgotten ...place?

ALLEN. Hey, that was very good.

CARMEN. What?

ALLEN. Weren't you trying to start every word with an "f?"

CARMEN. No. Why would I do that?

ALLEN. I don't know. I just thought...

CARMEN. Oh, I see. You're one of those guys that sits back and analyzes people, right? The kind of guy that puts people on pins like moths or butterflies and examines them. The kind that doesn't get involved. That right?

ALLEN. No. Actually I can get very involved with people. Sometimes I get so involved I forget who I am and I lose myself in other people's lives, kind of blend in, you know, and I become them and they become me and then I'm not me any more, I'm them and they're me and then I'm not sure who I am and I'm not even sure what I'm saying, or if I'm saying. *(beat)* Do you know what I'm saying?

CARMEN. *(casually)* Oh, sure. Happens to me all the time.

*(**ALLEN** looks relieved and moves closer to speak confidentially.)*

ALLEN. Want to hear a secret?

CARMEN. No.

ALLEN. Never told anyone before.

CARMEN. No, no, no.

ALLEN. Why?

CARMEN. I hate secrets. You tell me a secret then I feel all this pressure to keep it. It's too much responsibility. I can't handle it.

ALLEN. Okay, okay, it's not a secret. Can I tell you now?

CARMEN. *(pause to think)* Okay.

ALLEN. I sit here every day. From ten in the morning to four in the afternoon, then again from six in the evening to ten at night. Every day. Ten to four, then six to ten. And I wait. I drink my coffee, eat my Danish, and I patiently wait.

CARMEN. What happens between four and six?

ALLEN. *(puzzled)* Good question. I'm not sure. Nothing, I think. I think I just sit at home. I do a lot of sitting. *(starts slowly then increases in passion.)* See, I know that sooner or later someone is going to walk through that door. Someone is coming in here and my life is going to change. And when they do, boy oh boy, then things are going to be great. I'm going to be a different person, I'm going to leave this place, I'm going to experience life to the max. I'm going to set the world on fire, I'm going to grab the world by the balls and squeeze until I can't squeeze any more. I'm going right to the top, babe. And that's why when this girl, this Carmen, walked in I said to myself, Allen, she's someone to get involved with.

CARMEN. *(flattered, smiling)* Really?

ALLEN. Absolutely. I can get very involved.

CARMEN. *(snarling)* Well, I don't trust people that want to get involved with me so back off, buddy. Stand clear. Get too close to me and I'll rip your face off. *(beat)* Still don't think I'm messed up?

ALLEN. Not at all. Actually, I think you have a certain...a certain...

CARMEN. Charm?

ALLEN. Uh, uh. I'd call it more of a fascination. That's it. It's like I'm waiting to see what will happen next.

(CARMEN now becomes increasingly angry, but ALLEN, unaware of this, becomes increasing excited with the imagery.)

CARMEN. Like an amusement.

ALLEN. Yeah, that's it. Like being on a roller coaster.

CARMEN. Like I'm a ride.

ALLEN. Yeah, yeah, a ride. Maybe even like sitting in a car heading for a cliff.

CARMEN. I see. Now I'm an exciting car wreck.

ALLEN. *(starts slowly and builds momentum, in tune with the car)* Oh, man, you bet. You know when you're in a car and you're barreling down a country road at two in the morning at eighty miles an hour and it's pitch black out and there's a mist on the road and your headlights don't go more than thirty feet in front of you and you're driving nearly blind and you know this may be the last car ride you'll ever take, or this may be the last breath you'll ever draw, or this may be the last thing you'll ever do and you don't give a shit because the crazy person behind the wheel is you and your brain is fried with having taken every fucking pill ever created and you press the gas even further to the floor and you get so high you start to scream with excitement until your lungs are going to burst? You know how that is?

CARMEN. *(beat)* No.

ALLEN. I think I wet my pants.

CARMEN. I think I'm out of here.

ALLEN. No, wait.

CARMEN. Wait? Fuck you, wait. This happens to me all the time. No matter where I go I always run into freaks like you. Coffee, Danish, you look easy, mild, meek, somebody I could hang with, someone who would help me straighten out. Instead I meet disgusting freaks like you. Creep.

(CARMEN grabs the two dollars from the table and exits in a rush. ALLEN yells after her.)

ALLEN. Does that mean I won't be seeing you again?

(ALLEN dejectedly returns to his coffee and Danish. After a few beats, CARMEN slowly re-enters, returns to the table and sits.)

ALLEN. *(calls off stage)* Ed, two more coffees and Danish. *(CARMEN nudges ALLEN to remind him)* And Ed, no prune.

THE END

PROPERTY

Coffee cup
Cherry Danish on plate
Knife
Fork
Napkin
Cell phone
2 dollar bills
4 quarters

COSTUME

CARMEN:
Short skirt
Boots
Fishnet stocking (if available)

ALLEN:
Pants too short
White socks

MORNING COFFEE

CAST

ED

DEBBY

PETE

SETTING: Two tables, four chairs.

AT LIGHTS: **PETE** *sits alone at a table reading a news-paper.*

*(***ED*** *enters. He stares for a beat at* **PETE,** *but neither react.* **ED** *takes a seat at a table at a distance from* **PETE** *and opens his newspaper.* **DEBBY** *enters and approaches* **ED**'s *table with a cup and pot of coffee.* **ED** *doesn't look up, keeps reading.* **DEBBY** *stands and waits. Still* **ED** *doesn't look up.)*

DEBBY. *(bored beyond belief)* Morning. The usual?

ED. *(barely glancing her way)* Yeah, morning Deb. The usual would be fine, thanks.

*(***DEBBY** *mechanically pours the coffee then heads off.* **ED** *doesn't look up when* **DEBBY** *returns carrying a plate of toast. She wipes her eyes. She stands in front of him, smiling weakly, expectantly.* **ED** *lifts his cup and sees* **DEBBY***.)*

ED (CONT'D) What happened, Deb? You been crying?

DEBBY. It's this place. You guys **(DEBBY** *waves her arms around the stage as if encompassing other people)* come in every morning like clockwork. First that guy **(PETE)** over there, at seven-o-three. Then you, seven-fifteen, like clock-work. Every morning you guys sit in the same places, drink the same coffee, eat the same food, read the same papers. You been coming in now for what, two, three years. Every morning it's the same. "Morning, Deb," "The usual would be fine, thanks." Listen buddy, my name is Debby, not Deb. Debby. I also exist. Every morning you guys come in here and never talk, not to each other, not to me, not even to yourselves. I stand behind the counter and watch two guys read the paper and not even recognize that someone else is

19

alive in this place. There are times when I feel like setting fire to the newspapers or better yet to you. Yeah, I'm crying. It's this place. No, it's you guys. You're driving me nuts. And I don't even know your name. *(beat)* I said, I don't know your name. (beat, then hysterically at the top of her lungs) I SAID, I DON'T EVEN...

ED. Ed. It's Ed.

DEBBY. *(collapsing in relief)* Thank God.

(Long pause as **ED** *stares at* **DEBBY**. **PETE**, *watches, but never moves a muscle.)*

ED. Deb, oh, I'm sorry, Debby, Debby, right, Debby. Well, Debby, I'm sorry you feel that way, but I had no idea. I never meant any harm, but, you know, it's the morning and I'm not worth a damn in the morning. I don't know about the other guy, but for my part it'll never happen again. Never. I promise.

DEBBY. Thank you, Ed.

ED. You can take it to the bank, Debby.

*(***DEBBY*** exits.)*

(to **PETE***) The waitress in the diner just before I started coming here had the same reaction Deb just had, and it also took around three years. Know what I did?

*(***PETE*** doesn't react.)*

Same thing I'm going to do now. Lots of other diners in town, pal. Adios.

*(***ED*** throws money on the table, exits. **PETE** goes back to his newspaper. Lights down.)*

THE END

PROPERTY

2 cups
Plate
Toast
Coffee pot
2 newspapers
3 dollar bills

COSTUME

Waitress apron

HIERARCHY

CAST

JIM

MEL

SETTING: Two tables, four chairs.

AT LIGHTS: **JIM** *seated holding a cup.* **MEL** *enters with cup and sits with* **JIM**.

MEL. Watcha get?

JIM. Chai tea.

MEL. What the fuck is chai tea?

JIM. Idonknow. Tea made from chai's, I guess. I never know what to order in these places. What you get?

MEL. Espresso. Neat, straight up.

JIM. Too much for me, that stuff. Take the hair off your head.

MEL. You look like shit.

JIM. It's Gloria.

MEL. *(sniffs)* No. It's shit all right. Gloria doesn't smell like that.

JIM. No fucking jokes, okay, Mel. I'm having a tough time here.

MEL. Sorry, Jimbo. So, Gloria.

JIM. Always busting my hump.

MEL. Yeah, I know.

JIM. What do you know?

MEL. That she's always busting your hump.

JIM. You seen it too, huh?

MEL. No. Fact is, I always thought she treated you better than you deserved.

JIM. Then why did you say she was always busting my hump?

MEL. I was just repeating what you said, Jimmy.

JIM. I thought you were agreeing.

MEL. Fact is, I don't agree. Like I said.

JIM. Better than I deserve? What's with that?

MEL. Hey, don't turn this into me and you, Jimmy. It's supposed to be you and Gloria, remember?

JIM. Works better for you that way, Mel? You like it better that way?

MEL. What the fuck, Jim? What's happenin' here?

JIM. I always knew you had a thing for Gloria.

MEL. Of course I got a thing for Gloria, but that's not the point, here. I just come in, see you looking like shit, I try to be wadda ya call it, supportive, and then you whack me with you thinking I got a thing for Gloria. I mean, please....

JIM. Don't "please" me you piece of shit.

MEL. Piece of shit? You miserable fucker. I don't care how long we know each other, you can't talk to me like that.

JIM. You been banging Gloria, is that it?

MEL. She tell you that?

JIM. Have you been banging Gloria? Speak up, shit head.

MEL. Hey, Jim boy, she is my fucking wife, right. I mean I got a right.

JIM. But she's seein' me, right. I mean I got a right, too, right?

MEL. Yeah, I guess, but you gotta look at the hierarchy of competing rights here.

JIM. *(backing off)* That's a point.

MEL. Sure. I think marriage tops just seein'.

JIM. Tops? Like scissor cuts paper, rock breaks scissor.

MEL. Paper covers rock. Like that. There's a hierarchy.

JIM. And...

MEL. Marriage tops seein', like I said. But seein' tops just being a social-type friend, like at a bar or something.

JIM. So you're saying you're still cool with all this.

MEL. As long as we understand the hierarchy.

JIM. The alpha male thing.

MEL. Exactly. Top dog.

JIM. I'm glad we straightened this out, Mel.

MEL. Now that we got it worked out, take my advice, Jimmy. Don't take Gloria personal. She breaks everyone's balls.

JIM. But she's a great lay, Mel.

THE END

PROPERTY

2 cups

HIM

CAST

RITA

JANET

SETTING: Table, two chairs.

AT LIGHTS: **RITA** *and* **JANET** *seated at table, cups in front of them.*

RITA. Why here?

JANET. This is where we met. At that table *(points)*. You were having a double frap with caramel. I saw you, came over, asked...

RITA. So this coffee, this meeting, is for the purpose of symmetry.

JANET. I just thought it would be a nice way of tying things up.

RITA. You mean tying me up and dropping me in the ocean.

JANET. I thought it would be nostalgic.

RITA. I thought you said we would still be friends.

JANET. I did say that and I meant that. Now I'm also saying something else.

RITA. What you're really saying is we can't be friends.

JANET. That's not what I'm saying, Rita.

RITA. But that's what you mean.

JANET. I can't help what you're hearing. What you are hearing is through angry ears. I'm saying and meaning just the opposite.

RITA. Okay, Janet, repeat it so I'm clear.

JANET. I'm saying we could still be friends, just not as close.

RITA. And close is what you don't want to be with me.

JANET. Now you've got it.

RITA. Is it because we slept together?

JANET. Of course not. That was great.

RITA. I always sensed some distance, but I never thought it was some morality thing.

JANET. There is no morality thing, Rita. I'm probably the least moral person you'll ever know.

RITA. Then what, Janet? Is it someone else?

JANET. Yes.

RITA. You were supposed to say no. Or at least lie.

JANET. Maybe I have some morality after all.

RITA. Hell of a time to find out. What's her name?

JANET. Him.

RITA. Her name is "Him?"

JANET. His name is Jake.

RITA. His name?

JANET. Jake.

RITA. I didn't know you...

JANET. Well I do.

RITA. But we...

JANET. I know. But with Jake, too. Funny, huh?

RITA. Somehow I don't see the humor.

JANET. I understand.

RITA. How long have you and Jake...?

JANET. Six months.

RITA. Six months? But you and I have only been dating two months.

JANET. And I enjoyed them, Rita.

RITA. So while I was...

JANET. So was Jake.

RITA. Does Jake know?

JANET. Of course not.

RITA. You are immoral.

JANET. See. I didn't lie about that.

RITA. I was a toy?

JANET. We were for each other, Rita. This wasn't one way.

RITA. But I thought...

JANET. I know, but I didn't.

RITA. You are such a snake.

JANET. I think we made each other happy. *(pause)* Was I wrong about that?

RITA. No, but you're not making me very happy now.

JANET. I know, but it's just time to move on.

RITA. With Jake.

JANET. Right.

RITA. What's he got that I haven't...

JANET. Can I get you a re-fill? A latté or something?

RITA. Don't get so nervous. I didn't mean anatomically.

JANET. Sorry. This isn't as easy as I thought it would be.

RITA. No, of course it's not easy. We're not doing Noel Coward, here, Janet. More like Hank Meyerson.

JANET. You mean two people sitting around a coffee shop trading intimacies while verbally dueling.

RITA. Right, but somehow, right now, I don't feel very intimate.

JANET. I'd like to hear more dueling from you though, Rita. I know you're hurt.

RITA. You want more dueling? Okay, how's this? Fuck you and fuck Jake. Forget the last part. You're already doing that.

JANET. I can't do this.

RITA. Then leave.

JANET. I can't do that either.

RITA. Ha! The snake is squirming.

(**JANET** *gets up to leave.*)

Sit down.

(**JANET** *sits.*)

I wish the rest was as easy as that was.

JANET. Have you ever been through something like this?

RITA. That's irrelevant. *(pause)* Yes.

JANET. Me, too.

RITA. *(tentatively)* How did it end?

JANET. Which one?

RITA. Are you fucking kidding me?

JANET. I told you I was immoral.

RITA. You would drop someone like me for a Jake?

JANET. Sometimes I drop a Jake for a Rita.

RITA. You've hurt a lot of people, Janet.

JANET. I guess the moral is don't get picked up in a coffee house.

RITA. You're a predator.

JANET. And you?

RITA. Bait.

JANET. I know that. I meant how did yours end.

RITA. *(pause)* Which one?

JANET. You hypocrite.

RITA. Bait have rights, too.

JANET. Were you the dropper or the dropee?

RITA. Couple of each.

JANET. So sometimes you're the predator, sometimes the bait.

RITA. Keeps it interesting.

JANET. The truth. Did you know this would end?

RITA. No. I thought this was really "it."

JANET. You probably thought each one was really "it."

RITA. More or less.

JANET. Did you know about Jake?

RITA. You blind-sided me with that one, kiddo. Are you going to tell him?

JANET. About you?

RITA. About us, Janet. There maybe a Jake, but there was an us.

JANET. If he asks.

RITA. You mean if he says, "Oh, by the way, Janet, did you ever have sex with a woman named Rita?"

JANET. Right. Otherwise, it stays with me.

RITA. And me. Remember me? For now at least, it also stays with me.

JANET. What does that mean?

RITA. Oh, you remember. There maybe a Jake, but there was an us. You know, me and you and a secret makes three.

JANET. I don't like your tone.

RITA. Tough shit.

JANET. You're threatening me?

(RITA *doesn't answer.*)

You're better than this.

RITA. No, I'm not. I may not be at the point of doing a Fatal Attraction deal and boiling your bunny, but right now I feel capable of kicking it around the block a few times.

JANET. To the point of telling Jake?

RITA. Do I know him?

JANET. No.

RITA. You said that a little too quickly. You were ready for me to ask, weren't you?

JANET. Not at all.

RITA. I bet I do know him.

JANET. Before we get to twenty-questions, I'm leaving.

(JANET *rises to leave.*)

RITA. He's the guy you told me about from work, the guy you never named. Am I right? I am right. Look how upset you are. Ha!

(JANET *sits.*)

You are so fucking transparent.

JANET. Are you sure, bait?

RITA. Don't call me bait.

JANET. Are you sure I'm all that transparent? If I am, how come I was able to mess around with you, huh bait?

RITA. Stop it.

JANET. You think you can threaten me? You think you'll tell Jake and then we go back to playing patty-cake? Not a fucking chance, bait.

RITA. I'm warning you to stop it, Janet.

JANET. Janet? Who the fuck is Janet? I'm a predator, remember. You think I'd give you my real name? You think anything I told you is real. Not only are you bait, but you are also a fool.

(**RITA** *pulls a knife out of her purse.*)

What the hell you think you're doing with that?

RITA. Bait? Fool? You lying bitch. I'll show you who's a fool.

(*Long pause. Tension is gone. They relax, sip their coffee. It is quickly clear they were role-playing.*)

How'd you like that?

JANET. Not bad. Let's call this scenario "Him."

RITA. Tell me again why you insist on role playing our break-up. I don't get it.

JANET. Don't you?

THE END

PROPERTY

2 cups
Sharp knife

BETTY

A MONOLOGUE

SETTING: Two tables, four chairs.

AT LIGHTS: **BETTY** *is seated at a table, cup in her hand.*

BETTY. Hey, buddy. *(beat)* Yeah, you. Buy me a latté. *(beat)* No? *(looks around)* How about you, pal? I'll sing you a song. Song for a latté, how about it? *(sings)* "I love java, I love tea. I love the java jive and...and..." How does that song go? Wait, wait, don't go. How about a story? Story of my life? *(beat)* Tell ya what. Buy me a latté and I'll tell ya a story ya ain't goin' believe. *(beat)* Story first? Ah, you're full of shit. I tell and you'll split. *(beat)* You promise, huh. *(beat)* Trust ya? As far as I can throw... Wait, hold on, hon, I'll tell ya. Don't go running off all pissy-like. But you promise, right? Story. Latté. Okay. So... I'm maybe twelve, walking home through the park. 'Bout ten years ago. *(beat)* Okay, so fifteen years ago. Don't be a wise guy. So, I'm walking through the park one night...*(beat)* Yeah, I know it's dangerous, but that's where I live. *(beat)* No, man, not on the other side of the park. In the park, back in the shrubs. Look, let's get on with this 'cause I need that latté, okay? Okay. So I'm headin' through the park and I spot this cup, see, and it looks like latté, so... *(beat)* No, no label, but that never stopped me. If it looks like java, I suck it down, you dig? I can't even begin to list all the shit I've swallowed. Okay, so up to the lips, down the pipe and bam. I mean, like slam bam. Like my fuckin' head is going to explode. Then, then, now here's the part that no one believes. Ready? I start shrinking. No, listen. No bullshit. Shrinking. I get down to the size of a gerbil's dingus. Small, man. *(beat)* You ever been that small? *(beat)* Then how do you know how it felt? Fact is, it scared the dooky out of me, pal. I mean, I'm looking at sparrows in a whole new way, you dig?

Then, now here's where it really gets interesting, then, I spot this white rabbit boppin' along holding a pocket watch. *(beat)* No shit, my man. Checkin' out the time. And dressed real spiffy, too. Anyway, he spots me and I'm like, "Oh, oh, do rabbits eat meat?" But, as you can see, he don't eat ol' Betty because ol' Betty is still here. Yes, she is and she is thirsty, pal. How about a little taste now? *(beat)* Tough guy, huh. Okay. So, the rabbit, the rabbit, see, checks his watch and starts chattering about being late. *(beat)* Yeah, is that somethin'? An English speaking rabbit. Go figure. Anyway he grabs my arm and jumps into this hole in the ground dragging me with him. I am freaking out. I figure dead for sure, right, or at least rape. So we hit the bottom and... now if you think the rabbit was weird, you gotta hear this shit. So I hit the bottom and there are these playing cards and... *(beat)* playing cards. You know, queen, king, jack, like that. *(beat)* Like what I'm saying, man, playing cards and these cards are swinging pelicans or flamingos or some big stupid lookin' birds...what's the bird that's pink? *(beat)* That's the baby. Pink flamingos. *(beat)* I don't know what makes 'em pink. Who cares? Let me finish here, okay. *(beat)* Thank you. So, these playing cards are using the pink flamingos as mallets to whack these rats that are like rolled up like balls. *(beat)* I don't know. Some kind of game. Tell you the skinny, pal, frankly I didn't give a shit what kind of game they was at, I wanted out of there. *(beat)* How'd I get out? Pay me the latté first, then...*(beat)* Chaotic? Bet your ass it was chaotic. But chaotic can be good, pal. Chaotic cleans out your head, drains your sinuses, flushes out your bowels. Chaos gets you away from all this *(waves her hand around)*, all this crap and you can start over, clean. Clean. And then, then you can slowly start moving back to wired. Wired is also good. In fact, wired is the whole point. So ol' Betty goes from chaos to wired. *(holds up cup)* This is wired. Pay me.

THE END

PROPERTY

Cup

THIS HAS BEEN SOME DAY

THIS HAS BEEN SOME DAY premiered at Avery Point Play-house, 1999, directed by James Alexander Bond. It was presented at The Producers Club, 2000, again directed by James Alexander Bond, Midtown International Theatre Festival, 2000, directed by Charles Armesto, Chatham Community Players, 2006, directed by Jon DeAngelis.

CAST

KAREN

MARVIN

HARVEY

ETHEL, mother of the above siblings.

SETTING: Two tables, four chairs.

AT LIGHTS: **KAREN**, **MARVIN**, **HARVEY** *and* **ETHEL** *sit at a table in a state of despair and lethargy which is initially reflected in their speech. Cups of coffee sit on the table, untouched.*

KAREN. This has been some day.

MARVIN. What?

HARVEY. She said this has been some day.

MARVIN. *(annoyed)* I didn't hear her, okay?

HARVEY. Don't get snappy. And you should have know what she said. She's been saying the same damn thing all day. *(imitating* **KAREN***)* This has been some day. This has been some day.

KAREN. Now who's getting snappy?

ETHEL. Please don't start arguing, Karen. This has been some day and I'm pooped.

KAREN. I'm not arguing. It's just that Harvey always tells people not to be snippy when he's the one that's always snippy.

HARVEY. I said snappy, not snippy.

KAREN. What's the difference?

HARVEY. Between snappy and snippy? A world of difference. A woooorld of difference.

MARVIN. *(to Karen)* Did you notice how often he repeats himself?

KAREN. Of course. Then he accuses me. But did you notice how often you snip at Harvey?

MARVIN. I do not.

KAREN. You do. You snip.

HARVEY. Snap.

KAREN. Snip.

HARVEY. Snap

ETHEL. Karen, stop picking on Marvin. He's a little upset today.

KAREN. Well, hell, so am I. It's not every day your father gets buried, you know.

HARVEY. Is that what's bothering you? The burial?

KAREN. Don't you think that's enough?

HARVEY. Since you two had a lousy relationship when he was alive, I don't see why his burial would bother you.

KAREN. Whether or not I had a good relationship with him is beside the point.

MARVIN. No, Karen, that is the point. I think what Harvey is saying is you're a hypocrite. Isn't that right, Harvey?

HARVEY. Poor Marvin. As usual you're not even close. I meant it seemed odd because before Dad died he told me he didn't really like Karen.

ETHEL. He never said that.

HARVEY. He did. Last month. He and I were sitting on the porch chatting about cannibalism. He leaned over and whispered in my ear, "You know, Harvey, I never cared much for Karen." Then he winked and laughed.

KAREN. He said that?

ETHEL. He mentioned cannibalism?

MARVIN. Did he mean he didn't like Karen as a person or as a food?

ETHEL. He never said that.

KAREN. He said that?

HARVEY. Don't forget that he winked and laughed.

ETHEL. *(befuddled)* He was talking about cannibalism?

KAREN. *(sarcastic)* I won't forget. Sounds like the best part.

ETHEL. He promised me he would never talk about the cannibalism.

HARVEY. It was always obvious to me he didn't care for you, especially once you came out.

ETHEL. Came out? You mean on the porch?

MARVIN. The closet, Ma.

ETHEL. Why was Karen in the closet?

KAREN. Well, I don't believe he said that. *(meaningfully)* He used to like me plenty.

HARVEY. *(defiant)* When?

KAREN. When I was little and he would come into my room at night. I sure found out about men then.

ETHEL. Wasn't it a nice funeral? So many people.

MARVIN. *(to Karen)* Don't be so conceited that Dad came into your room.

KAREN. Why not?

ETHEL. Why do you think there were so many young women at the funeral?

MARVIN. Just don't be so conceited, that's all.

ETHEL. And all those young women were just crying their eyes out. Who were they?

KAREN. Did he go into your room, too?

MARVIN. Just don't be so cocky, that's all. He got to know me really well, too.

(HARVEY clears his throat. KAREN and MARVIN now both slowly turn to look at HARVEY who slowly smiles and nods his head.)

HARVEY. *(smug)* Sometimes I went into his room.

ETHEL. And the way the chapel laid him out. He looked so life-like.

KAREN. *(to HARVEY)* When?

HARVEY. Whenever Mom was supposedly out bowling. Dad's door was always open for me. And then later we'd wait up for the cops to pour her under the door.

ETHEL. They never poured me under the door. *(all stare at her)* Well, maybe occasionally.

MARVIN. Can you imagine how busy he'd be at night if he had more kids? A real Max Sennett comedy. In this door, out that door. Busy, busy, busy. Good thing there were only the three of us.

(Becoming agitated, **ETHEL** *pulls a flask from her purse.)*

ETHEL. Is there any gin left?

KAREN. You've had enough.

*(***ETHEL*** turns the flask upside down to show it is empty.)*

ETHEL. *(becoming agitated)* Gin, gin, I need gin. Hurry.

KAREN. *(catching on there is more here than first thought.)* Wait. There were just the three of us, right Mom? I mean, you did have only three children.

*(***ETHEL*** counts those present.)*

ETHEL. Three children? One, two, three. Yes. There are three of you.

HARVEY. Karen means are there any more of us...

KAREN. ...or any less of us?

HARVEY. ...or anything we don't know about?

ETHEL. In this coffee shop?

KAREN. Anywhere.

ETHEL. Anywhere?

MARVIN. Ever.

ETHEL. *(after some thought)* Do Siamese twins count as one or two?

KAREN. You gave birth to Siamese twins?

ETHEL. Siamese twins are wonderful, don't you think? Two hearts that beat as one. Or in some cases, two heads that think as one.

HARVEY. Did you give birth to Siamese twins?

ETHEL. Just once.

*(***HARVEY***, **KAREN** and **MARVIN**, stunned, sit and stare at ***ETHEL***.)*

You don't have to look so stunned.

ALL. Yes we do.

ETHEL. Well, maybe, but don't blame Siam. It's a lovely country. Siam had nothing to do with it. *(beat)* In our case they should be called Burmese twins.

MARVIN. They were born in Burma?

KAREN. I never knew you lived in Burma.

ETHEL. Just for a few years. Until the heat died down here in the States. And Karen, I wouldn't be too upset about what Harvey said.

KAREN. You mean about Dad not liking me?

ETHEL. Well, the joke is on Harvey, because if your father didn't like you, then he certainly didn't like Harvey, either. What surprised me was that neither of you ever developed a Burmese accent.

HARVEY. You're saying we were the Siamese...

ETHEL. At the head.

HARVEY. Me and...

ETHEL. Karen

KAREN. For...

ETHEL. Two years.

*(Both **HARVEY** and **KAREN** feel their heads.)*

MARVIN. But I wasn't...

ETHEL. They threw you in.

MARVIN. I was thrown in?

ETHEL. Some sort of contest between Siam and Burma for whoever would have the twins first that year. *(proud)* I did, so I got the prize.

MARVIN. I was a prize? Like from a box of Cracker Jacks.

ETHEL. Actually. Siam was sick of the notoriety, so we got you from Siam for the twins being born in Burma.

MARVIN. I was a reward for not being born in Siam?

ETHEL. Think of it as being able to make a whole country happy.

HARVEY. Then he's not even our natural...

ETHEL. We adopted him fair and square. Poor little tyke wrapped in that blanket in the rice paddy.

MARVIN. *(starting to whine)* I was an abandoned baby you found in a rice paddy in Burma?

ETHEL. Good thing we got there when we did. The fucking ox almost stepped on you. Tell you the truth, the Siamese thought you had been stepped on by the ox, so they were pretty glad to get rid of you.

MARVIN. I was a booby prize.

HARVEY. Could we get back to the Siamese-Burmese- twin thingy business. At the head, attached, together, two hearts that beat as one?

ETHEL. In this case...

HARVEY. Two heads that think as one.

KAREN. I'm not sure I want to know.

HARVEY. But aren't Siamese-Burmese-twins of the same sex?

ETHEL. *(with great reluctance)* Wellll, yes.

KAREN. So then at one time we were both...then one of us was...altered?

ETHEL. Maybe we're dwelling too much in the past.

HARVEY. Listen, mother, I think we have a right to know which of us was...

KAREN. Doesn't matter. She loved me the best, didn't you, mother?

HARVEY. Loved you? You're crazy. When they separated us, I must have gotten all the brains.

KAREN. Just the part that makes your mouth move.

MARVIN. I feel left out. Are there ever Siamese triplets?

ETHEL. Well, I loved you all. Of course, your father wanted you all killed. *(laughs)* Thank God we were Catholic.

KAREN. We're not. We're Episcopalian.

ETHEL. Back then we were Catholic. Now we're Episcopalian. See?

HARVEY. No.

ETHEL. Of course, if we had stayed in Burma we would have remained Buddhist. Such a lovely place. Except for the fucking oxen and the CIA.

HARVEY. Why did you wait to tell us all this stuff?

ETHEL. We would have told you sooner, but the CIA, well, you know how those people are.

MARVIN. I don't believe it. CIA?

HARVEY. Now you're going to tell us Dad was a spy.

ETHEL. Counter.

HARVEY. Not for our side?

ETHEL. It was the only way to get out of Mongolia.

KAREN. Why did you have to get out of Mongolia?

ETHEL. Your father had a problem with one of the yaks.

MARVIN. *(close to hysteria)* I don't want to know.

ETHEL. It was perfectly innocent. He got drunk one night and wandered into the wrong building. Turned out to be the barn. Could have happened to anyone. And besides, he paid for the delivery. It's not that he just walked out on the poor beast. But I'll tell you, it's disgraceful over there. No medical insurance, no veterinarians, awful. Promise me you'll never go to Mongolia. Promise.

ALL. *(befuddled; resigned; sarcastic)* We promise.

HARVEY. And if I ever do, I promise not to have sex with a yak.

ETHEL. You all make me so proud to be your...your, er... well, your...

(ALL wait as ETHEL searches for the right word. As time passes they become increasingly desperate for ETHEL's word. Eventually, they all stand exit muttering good-byes, questions about their parent's mental health. We dimly hear "Yak," "CIA," "Twins," "They're both nuts," etc. Finally alone, ETHEL pulls another flask from her purse, pours some into her coffee, and takes a long drink.)

ETHEL (CONT'D) *(to audience)* God, this has been some day.

THE END

PROPERTY

4 cups

Hip flask

CLASS

CAST

ERNIE

ROXANNE

SETTING: Two tables, four chairs.

AT LIGHTS: **ERNIE** *sits at a table with a cup of coffee. He is reading the Racing Form. He alternates reading his newspaper with looking at his watch and then looking around as if waiting for someone. Finally, he carefully folds the newspaper and speaks to the audience in a heavy Brooklyn accent.*

ERNIE. *(to AUDIENCE)* I was supposed to meet Morty here about eleven and then head over to the track to play the ponies. Only now it's past eleven-thirty and still no Morty. Very unreliable guy, that Morty. I'm just lettin' ya know, ya know.

(Off-stage we hear **ROXANNE**'*s voice. It is coarse, loud and grating: Brooklynese with a cold.* **ERNIE** *stops to listen.)*

ROXANNE (O.S.) Look, I bought this cup of coffee and I'm drinking it and I gotta tell ya this stuff tastes like...

*(***ERNIE** *covers his ears, turns to the voice to check it out.)*

ERNIE. *(to AUDIENCE)* Whoa, that's some voice. Stop traffic with a voice like that. *(turns to direction of voice)* It's that babe over there hasslin' about the coffee. What she expect in a joint like this, champaign? Anyway, about Morty. *(sees something coming)* Oh, man. The babe with the voice is coming over. I feel a head-ache comin'.

*(***ROXANNE** *enters holding a cup of coffee. After looking around, she stops at Ernie's table.)*

ROXANNE. *(In a theatrically affected, cultured sounding, Queen of England voice)* Excuse me. Is this seat vacant? All the others appear to be taken.

ERNIE. What? Oh, no.

ROXANNE. Do you mind?

ERNIE. Me? Nah. I was just gonna leave anyway.

ROXANNE. Oh, don't leave on my account. Perhaps I should wait for another table.

ERNIE. *(to AUDIENCE)* Don't leave on my account. Perhaps I should wait for another table. You get that? This babe with a voice that could stop traffic suddenly drops this Queen of England stuff on me and I'm, like, WHAT? Before she sounded like she was sellin' fish, now she sounds like little silvery chimes. *(to* **ROXANNE***)* No problem. It's my pleasure. Have a seat.

*(***ROXANNE*** *sits.)*

(to AUDIENCE) You get that? It's my pleasure. First time in my life, I swear, I ever put those three words together. It's my pleasure. I don't even know what that means. How do I know it's my pleasure? I mean, I might have just given half my table to a leper. For all I know, I can lose a finger or a nose or somethin'. Or maybe she's some crazy that'll go for my throat.

*(***ROXANNE*** *starts to rummage around in her purse and pulls out a beat-up book, sips her coffee and starts to read.* **ERNIE** *starts to sip his coffee and also starts to read his Racing Form, but is obviously distracted by* **ROX-ANNE** *and, after a few moments, gives the reading up as hopeless. As the following unfolds,* **ROXANNE***'s speech gradually moves from sounding like the Queen of England, to sounding like* **ERNIE***.)*

ERNIE (CONT'D) I see you're readin'. Don't mean to disturb you, but who's this guy Fraud your readin'?

ROXANNE. Freud, not fraud.

ERNIE. Did I say fraud? Ha. I meant Freud. That's funny, right? *(beat)* So, who is this guy? Give me a clue.

ROXANNE. *(Looking at* **ERNIE** *as if he were hanging on a wall in a museum)* I don't think you'd understand it.

ERNIE. No, no, go ahead. Try me.

ROXANNE. Well, this Freud guy, he says that we're doing things all the time that we don't know we're doing.

ERNIE. Like we're in a fog, or somethin'.

ROXANNE. More like we got a little guy inside of us that pulls the strings.

ERNIE. Hey, I got a little guy in my pants that pulls the strings. That what he means?

ROXANNE. Exactly the point. That's our id. Hey, you're pretty sharp. And then there's another little guy in us that makes us feel guilty.

ERNIE. Must be my mother. She could make Don Corleone feel guilty.

ROXANNE. Hey. You sure you never read this stuff?

ERNIE. Scout's honor. *(to AUDIENCE)* Right, like I'm going to be found dead readin' this kind of shit.

ROXANNE. Me, personally, I'm very interested in Freud. He speaks to me, you know? It makes me think I would make a good therapist.

ERNIE. Therapist? Like when my father hurt his back he went to this therapist to help him walk better and then screw the insurance company.

ROXANNE. Like that, except this is for your head.

ERNIE. *(suddenly enlightened)* Oh, a head doctor.

ROXANNE. Yeah, that's it. I think I'd be good at it, too. Hey, who knows, maybe I can help you.

ERNIE. *(disdainfully dismissive)* You help me? You help me? You kidding or somethin'?

ROXANNE. You know, I read where the people most in need of help are those who say they don't need any help.

ERNIE. Oh, I need help. I need help, okay. I need help with the fourth race today at the track. Think you can help me with that, Miss Doc?

ROXANNE. No, Mister Wise-Guy. I don't know anything about horses. But I think I'm pretty good at people. Like the time I helped out Marie, my friend, beautician and manicurist.

*(During the following, **ROXANNE** mimes talking to **ERNIE**.)*

ERNIE. *(to AUDIENCE)* So this babe wants me to spill my feelings about this and that, tell her, a total stranger, all about my inner me. I don't think so. I mean, what's in it for me, you know. Still, she does seem really interested and that don't happen every day, at least to me. So what the...

ROXANNE. *(continuing)* ...and the next thing you know, Marie and her family all go down to Miami for a vacation together. Happy as clams.

ERNIE. Whoa, listen, I'll tell you about me and my parents and my inner self if you promise I don't have to go down to Miami. I hate to sweat and there's only one decent race track. It's a nightmare down there.

ROXANNE. Yeah, yeah, I promise. So now, your parents. What about 'em?

ERNIE. What a pair they are. Always on my back. They're killers.

ROXANNE. They got a beef with you, huh?

ERNIE. Aw, it's about my work.

ROXANNE. They don't like your work?

ERNIE. They got nothin' to like or not like. Right now I don't have work. And my laying off really strung out my father. The other day he says to me, he says, listen to this, if Babe Ruth was the Sultan of Swat, I'm the Sultan of Sloth. I had to look that sloth up in a dictionary. Is that unreal or what? That's my old man.

ROXANNE. Sounds like my mother. Always got your head in a book, she says. Always readin'.

*(During the following, **ROXANNE** mimes talking to **ERNIE**.)*

ERNIE. *(to AUDIENCE)* Boy, that was quick. She tells me to talk about me and then she moves to the rail and starts racing me toward the finish line. I thought therapists are supposed to listen to other people, not flap their own gums. Maybe she ain't all that interested.

ROXANNE. *(continuing)* ...I'm lookin' to improve myself and she beats on me. My mother. Piece of work. *(beat)* You know, you seem like a smart guy. You been to college?

ERNIE. Yeah, I gave it a tumble.

ROXANNE. *(Skeptical)* Oh, yeah? Which one?

ERNIE. The one over cross town. The big one.

ROXANNE. Oh, that one. Yeah, I passed it a couple of times. Big.

ERNIE. Yeah. I walked in, walked out. Too spooky that place. *(to* **ROXANNE***)* So what's ya name?

ROXANNE. Hey, just because we're talkin' college don't mean I gotta give ya my name.

ERNIE. First of all we ain't talking college, we're talking families. Second of all, you givin' me your name don't mean I'm poppin' the question. Right?

*(**ROXANNE***'s thinking this over becomes a production, an event, like her voice. First she bites her lip, then she sips her coffee, she messes with her book, she diddles with her hair.* **ERNIE** *sits enthralled.)*

ERNIE (CONT'D) *(to AUDIENCE)* Is this is a circus, or what? If I knew it would be so entertaining, I would have asked a really tough question like her address.

ROXANNE. *(reluctantly)* Okay, it's Roxanne.

ERNIE. Hey, Roxanne. Nice name. Foreign, huh?

ROXANNE. How'd you know it was foreign?

ERNIE. I know because my favorite film of all time is Cyrano what's his face. The guy with the big nose. The babe in that one, her name is Roxanne and she's French.

ROXANNE. I'm very impressed. First ya caught on really quick about Freud, now you knew about my name.

ERNIE. Hey, ya learn things in life, ya know?

ROXANNE. Wow, you are a smart guy. I am really... *(groping for the word)*

ERNIE. Impressed?

ROXANNE. Exactly. And you're...?

ERNIE. Ernie. That's short for Ernest. That means honest and true blue. *(to AUDIENCE)* Between you and me, that means shit, but I been using that line for ten years, so what the hell, ya know?

ROXANNE. Nice to meet ya, Ernie.

ERNIE. No offense, Roxanne, but when you were gettin' your coffee you sounded like a train wreak. Then you come to the table and you sounded amazin'. Like the Queen of England. Now we're talkin' and you sound more normal, ya know?

ROXANNE. I'm studyin' to be an actress. That's part of my voice trainin'.

ERNIE. No shit.

ROXANNE. Swear.

ERNIE. No offense, but it sounded like bullshit to me.

ROXANNE. It is bullshit. That's why it's called actin'. In fact, that's why I'm here.

ERNIE. They puttin' on a show in the coffee shop?

ROXANNE. Nah. I'm waiting for my actin' teacher.

ERNIE. So you gonna be on Broadway, or what?

ROXANNE. Right now I think it's mostly "or what." I'm still learnin'. I'm like a starlet, ya know?

ERNIE. *(to AUDIENCE, excited)* Life's amazing, right? One minute I'm readin' the Racing Form, next I'm chatting up a starlet.

ROXANNE. I know you said you ain't working now, this minute, but when you do work, what kind of work do you do?

ERNIE. Ya know, Roxanne, I always hate that question mostly because I hate being labeled. I don't like bein' pigeon-toed, ya know.

ROXANNE. Oh, I couldn't agree more. *(pause)* So what kind of work do you do? When you work, I mean.

ERNIE. Well, right now I'm waitin' for the right thing, ya know? I had a bunch of jobs, but nothin' really appealed to me so now I'm layin' back, figurin' my options.

ROXANNE. It's good you can afford to do that. You don't have to hustle your ass. Me, I gotta.

ERNIE. Gotta what?

ROXANNE. Hustle my ass.

ERNIE. See, I think "hustle my ass" doesn't sound right

comin' from you. A babe like you, a starlet, should stick with the refined speech you used before.

ROXANNE. Think so?

ERNIE. Definitely. It's got more class.

ROXANNE. Well, you should know, you being such a classy guy and all.

ERNIE. *(to AUDIENCE)* You hear that? She said I'm a classy guy? Up 'til now I was never really sure, ya know? I mean, I got the gold chains, the tan, the star sapphire pinkie ring, the clear nail polish, the whole nine yards. Still, there's always this doubt whether I had class, ya know. It sounded, I don't know, too snobby or somethin'. But now this babe with a name like Roxanne, this starlet actress takin' actin' lessons that reads stuff besides the Racing Form, she nails me. A classy guy. Have you noticed that this babe has gotten better lookin'. I wouldn't go so far as to say pretty. Nice is about it. Which for her ain't bad. I mean, ya gotta figure the distance a person has to travel, right? This is turnin' out okay, ya know?

ROXANNE. *(to AUDIENCE)* I'll tell you the way it is for me. I'm pushing thirty, and to be truthful, my date calendar ain't exactly crammed. Is Ernie the guy? Beats me. He's like a lot of guys I meet. Like that dick joke when I just sit down. Guaranteed someplace along the line I hear a dick joke. Can I see through the bullshit? Like a Windexed pane of glass. Horse player, probably never worked an honest job, but I've been there before with worse. And the more I've been sittin' here, the better he's been gettin'. Not a rave, but nice, you know. Which for him ain't bad. I mean, ya gotta figure the distance a person has to travel, right. This is turnin' out okay, ya know?

(**ROXANNE** *turns to* **ERNIE.** *They look at each other a short while before they smile at each other and the lights fade to black.*

THE END

PROPERTY

Racing Form newspaper
2 cups
Book with FREUD in large letters on cover

COSTUMES

Gold chain
Pinky ring
Overly large woman's handbag

HOPEFUL BETTY

CAST

BETTY

FREDDY

SETTING: Two tables, four chairs.

AT LIGHTS: **BETTY**, *holding coffee cup, talking on cell phone.*

BETTY. Look, Ma, I'm not over-joyed about this either, but I figure, why not. Cheryl, down at the office, she met this guy on the internet and it worked out great for her so I thought, hey, why not give it a try...Stop worrying, Ma. It's just a date. You really think I would just...Ma, please, give me more credit. I'm not that desperate... Two years...Okay, it's been three years, but that doesn't mean I would just jump into bed with...You know, I'm very upset you would bring that up and I'm also upset you'd have so little faith...I know that, but he said he was using a...I told you I'd pay you back, but things are tight...Well, it wasn't so pleasant for me either, you know. I mean, I'm the one who had the...Look, not only will I be more careful, Ma, but there will be nothing to be careful about.

*(**FREDDY** enters, looks around)*

BETTY. I think he's here. Gotta hang. Okay, I promise.

*(**FREDDY** walks to **BETTY**.)*

FREDDY. You Betty?

BETTY. Yeah.

FREDDY. I'm Freddy.

BETTY. Want some coffee.

FREDDY. No. Wanna fuck?

BETTY. Sure.

*(Lights snap off, then snap on. **BETTY** and **FREDDY** seated at the table.)*

BETTY. That was great. Wanna get married?

FREDDY. Sure.

(Lights snap off, then snap on. **BETTY** *and* **FREDDY** *seated at the table.)*

BETTY. Are you happy married to me?

FREDDY. No.

*(***FREDDY*** exits.* **BETTY** *makes a call.)*

BETTY. It's over...I don't know, he just wasn't happy... Of course we did "it." We were going to be married remember?...Just that one time, maybe twice, I don't remember...I don't know if I had a....and it's not really any of your business...Because it was over so quick... Both. When we did "it" and the relationship. Slam, bam and that was it...No, not even a thank you ma'am...I guess you're right. Two days isn't a very long time, but it's amazing how boring it could be...But you and Dad have been...Thirty-eight years? I thought it was thirty-four... But that's my point. I could see thirty-eight years being boring, but two days?...Miss him? It was only two days so what's to miss...Nah, I'm better off. He was too controlling, anyway...I don't think so, but you never know. He left his tooth-brush, so maybe...

THE END

PROPERTY

2 cups
Cell phone

GEORGE AND MARTHA
FIND A WAY

GEORGE AND MARTHA FIND A WAY premiered at Avery
Point Playhouse, 1999, directed by James Alexander Bond.
It was presented at The Producers Club, 2000, again
directed by James Alexander Bond, Midtown International
Theatre Festival, 2000, directed by Charles Armesto, and
New Jersey Dramatists, 2003, directed by John Peterson.

CAST

GEORGE

MARTHA

SETTING: Two tables, four chairs.

AT RISE: **GEORGE** *and* **MARTHA** *sit at a table, each with a cup of coffee.*

GEORGE. Nice place, Martha.

MARTHA. No big deal, George. We do grass, they do caffeine. Look at 'em, all wired, eyeballs lit up like bloodhounds. The way they're bouncing around here, they should pad the walls. Grass is much cooler.

GEORGE. Want some cake or something?

MARTHA. How come this sudden concern about me?

GEORGE. Shouldn't a husband be concerned about his loving wife? *(looking over her shoulder)* Oh, look, two chairs by the window. Wanna move?

MARTHA. I don't want to move. What I do want is for you to tell me what the hell is going on.

GEORGE. I have something to tell you.

MARTHA. I knew it.

GEORGE. I want a divorce.

MARTHA. *(quickly)* Okay.

GEORGE. What?

MARTHA. I said okay. What part of that didn't you understand?

GEORGE. The quickness.

MARTHA. So I'm decisive.

GEORGE. That's it?

MARTHA. I'm decisive and charming?

GEORGE. I meant is that all? You don't want to know why?

MARTHA. I know why I'm decisive and charming. I was raised right by my parents.

GEORGE. I meant...

MARTHA. *(smug)* I know what you meant. You thought I was going to be surprised, right? George, you haven't surprised me in fifteen years. I know what you're thinking, when you're going to act, the why, the how and the where. When you just started being nice to me before, I said to myself, Martha, George wants a divorce.

(With the following rapid interchange, **GEORGE** *becomes increasingly frustrated trying to compete with* **MARTHA***'s sagacity.* **MARTHA***, on the other hand, increasingly glows as she wins point after point.)*

GEORGE. Wanna know why George wants a divorce?

MARTHA. Because you're unhappy.

GEORGE. Wanna know why I'm unhappy?

MARTHA. Because you don't want to be tied down.

GEORGE. Wanna know why I don't want to be tied down?

MARTHA. Because you want to bring a freshness to your life.

GEORGE. Wanna know why I want to bring a freshness to my life?

MARTHA. *(the winning point)* Because you're unhappy. *(a triumphant pause)* That pretty much brings it full circle doesn't it, oh enlightened one?

(There is a pause as **GEORGE** *stares at* **MARTHA** *while she casually ignores him.)*

GEORGE. You know what this does to me.

MARTHA. You buy me a four dollar coffee that tastes like it was filtered through a sock, tell me you want a divorce and now expect me to feel sorry for you. George, you're predictable, but ballsy.

GEORGE. You know what this does to me.

MARTHA. I just said...

GEORGE. You know what this does to me when you get this way.

*(***MARTHA*** *looks initially puzzled, then slowly reacts.)*

MARTHA. Oh, that. Reeeally?

GEORGE. *(smiles at her)* You did this on purpose.

MARTHA. *(glances at* **GEORGE***'s crotch)* No, I swear. Did you...?

GEORGE. No, I managed to stop it before... If we were home...

MARTHA. That's sweet. And you said you wanted a divorce.

GEORGE. When you get like that I don't have any control over it.

MARTHA. George, you'd fuck a knot-hole in a rotting tree. You're corrupt.

GEORGE. *(leering)* I know.

MARTHA. Well, the divorce is still on.

GEORGE. Wait.

MARTHA. Wait your ass. No waiting. It's lawyer time.

GEORGE. Can't you take a joke?

MARTHA. Look, George, just because you get turned-on by some masochistic fantasy, don't think this is going to work out. You wanted it, you got it, babe.

GEORGE. I was just trying to get you going.

MARTHA. Bullshit.

GEORGE. You have no sense of humor, Martha, no sense of the new, of finding life in life. You're dead, Martha and I'm alive and live people don't want to be with dead people. So if it's divorce you want, it's divorce you'll get.

MARTHA. First of all, George, this was your idea. And second: no sense of humor? Me?

GEORGE. Yes, you, Martha. Here I set you up for a little joke and you go all serious on me. The only reason I suggested the possibility of maybe a divorce was to wake you up a little to our marriage, to our life. I'm trying to do you a favor, here, Martha.

MARTHA. Oh, that was good, George. Doing me a favor. You didn't think that up yourself, did you, George? Tell the truth, who wrote this for you? Come on. Who created the divorce sketch?

GEORGE. Spur of the moment.

MARTHA. Liar.

GEORGE. Maybe it was the caffeine.

MARTHA. Maybe it was all the young yuppie ass in this caffeine den that caught your attention.

GEORGE. Are you really going to...

MARTHA. What?

GEORGE. You know.

MARTHA. No, George, tell me. What?

GEORGE. Are you teasing me, again?

MARTHA. *(glancing at* **GEORGE***'s crotch)* Ask your dowser. It can pick up humiliation like radar picks up a missile.

GEORGE. I need an answer.

MARTHA. Let me ask you this, George. You've been complaining about my not bringing a spark to our marriage for the past, oh, five years or so. Right?

GEORGE. I guess five years is about right.

MARTHA. And in those five years have you ever, once, considered that I was perfectly happy with the way things were going?

GEORGE. Well, I...

MARTHA. That maybe I was perfectly content with the status quo?

GEORGE. No, I guess I...

MARTHA. That I didn't want the boat rocked?

GEORGE. No, you seemed...

MARTHA. No, George, not seemed. I was. I was perfectly content and perfectly happy to let things move along as they did. And you never asked why.

*(***GEORGE** *reacts with increasing passion.)*

GEORGE. Okay, why?

MARTHA. You were so caught up in your own little world, your own little obsessive concerns, you never looked at me and asked, why is Martha so content, so happy. Did you?

GEORGE. Okay, why?

MARTHA. Stared at your own navel, never giving my life even a fleeting thought, so wrapped up in your own misery.

GEORGE. Okay, why?

MARTHA. Never wondered once...

GEORGE. *(finally explodes)* OKAY. OKAY. WHY? TELL ME. NOW. WHY?

(MARTHA checks her nails.)

MARTHA. I was fucking Nick.

(GEORGE quickly grabs his crotch.)

Did that do it?

GEORGE. *(catching his breathe, then smiling)* Oooh, yeah.

(MARTHA, looking somewhat smug, sips her coffee, smiles at GEORGE.)

MARTHA. I still have the touch, right Georgie?

GEORGE. Baby, you're the best.

MARTHA. Thank you, Georgie. Tomorrow we'll hit the place on 74th Street. It has better coffee.

(GEORGE stands, holding a napkin over his crotch. She stands. They exit.)

THE END

PROPERTY

2 cups
2 napkins (large)

HAPPY BIRTHDAY

HAPPY BIRTHDAY premiered at Avery Point Playhouse, 1999, directed by James Alexander Bond. It was presented at The Producers Club, 2000, again directed by James Alexander Bond, and the Midtown International Theatre Festival, 2000, directed by Charles Armesto.

CAST

RICHIE

PAUL

SETTING: Two tables, four chairs.

AT LIGHTS: **PAUL** *seated at a table with cup of coffee reading his newspaper.* **RICHIE,** *coffee in hand, enters and sits with* **PAUL.**

RICHIE. It's going to be difficult to talk about this, Paul.

PAUL. *(reading the newspaper)* Uh huh.

RICHIE. No, I mean it. It is really frightening.

PAUL. *(still reading)* So just say it, Richie. It'll be okay.

RICHIE. I hate this. It sounds like I'm whining. Like I'm a baby.

PAUL. *(still reading)* I'm willing to feed you, Richie, but I'll be damned if I'll change your diaper.

RICHIE. Are you going to listen to me, or, as usual, bury yourself in the paper?

PAUL. I do not...well, yes I do, but that's because it's more interesting than you. Okay, what?

RICHIE. I saw something today that scared the shit out of me.

PAUL. Your bank account?

RICHIE. If you can't be serious, I'm leaving.

PAUL. I'm sorry. That's it. I got it out of my system.

RICHIE. You always do this. I try to be serious and you always have this glib jokey reaction.

PAUL. You're right, you're right. It's a tic. Kvetch away, Prince Mishkin.

RICHIE. I was walking down Columbus Avenue. There was a young couple, couldn't have been more than twenty, walking ahead of me, arms around each other. Then the guy, he reaches down and squeezes the girl's ass. *(beat)* That's it.

PAUL. *(puzzled)* Yeah. I can see how that would scare the shit

81

out of you. Squeezed her ass, huh? Has an alien twist to it.

RICHIE. You don't get it.

PAUL. Of course I don't get it. I'm married. Married guys never get it. Just ask their wives. *(in shrewish voice)* "You just don't get it, Paul."

RICHIE. Paul, when was the last time you squeezed a girl's ass?

PAUL. This morning.

RICHIE. Really?

PAUL. My daughter.

RICHIE. She's six.

PAUL. And very squeezable.

RICHIE. When was it, Paul?

PAUL. What are you getting at Richie? That you're frustrated at getting older? That life isn't treating you fairly? That you want blood to run in your dick instead of Freon?

RICHIE. All of the above.

PAUL. *(suddenly enlightened)* I know. It's your birthday, right? Aren't you forty next week?

RICHIE. Two weeks. And that's not the issue.

PAUL. That's not the issue? That's the very issue. You always get morbid around your birthday. This existential angst takes over. Get over yourself, Richie. Your life ain't that important.

RICHIE. You're wrong.

PAUL. About?

RICHIE. *(angry)* Everything.

PAUL. *(surprised and amused)* Well, this is different. I've never seen you so worked up.

RICHIE. You're memory is going. I told you before this was different.

PAUL. Actually, what you said was this was difficult, not different.

RICHIE. You're pulling your lawyer splitting hair bullshit with me and avoiding the issue.

PAUL. Which is?

RICHIE. Time.

PAUL. Your issue, not mine.

RICHIE. Ridiculous. Time is everybody's issue.

PAUL. Only for the terminally self-absorbed.

RICHIE. No, the reason you're not concerned with time is because your narcissism won't allow you to believe you're mortal.

PAUL. That's right. That's why we elite are called immortal.

RICHIE. Fact is, the only issue you have is superficial.

PAUL. What do you mean by that?

RICHIE. You just skim across the surface. You never look at yourself.

PAUL. I leave that to you. I figure sooner or later you'll tell me whatever I have to know. Easier that way. And I think I have an important issue.

RICHIE. Money?

PAUL. You think all I'm interested in is money?

RICHIE. Yes.

PAUL. It's that obvious, huh?

RICHIE. What's the first thing you think of when you wake up?

PAUL. Peeing.

RICHIE. Alright, second thing.

PAUL. More peeing.

RICHIE. What?

PAUL. I drank a lot the night before.

RICHIE. Second thing, Paul.

PAUL. Money.

RICHIE. Third thing?

PAUL. *(hesitant)* Money.

RICHIE. Last thing before you go to sleep. (*quickly before* **PAUL** *can answer*) After peeing.

PAUL. Money.

RICHIE. So congratulations on having a profoundly human issue which governs your life.

PAUL. What is this, issue snobbery? You worry about what you want, I'll worry about what I want.

RICHIE. But this money thing is just another example of the superficial way you handle everything. Even your friendships.

PAUL. Lie.

RICHIE. How long have I known you, Paul?

PAUL. Oh God, let's not make this overly dramatic, okay, Rich?

RICHIE. Twenty years.

PAUL. So?

RICHIE. Pretty long time, don't you think?

PAUL. I guess.

RICHIE. Don't you think that makes our relationship kind of special?

PAUL. *(sarcastic)* Are you upset because I forgot our anniversary? I forgot the flowers?

RICHIE. I'm upset because you don't take me seriously.

PAUL. That's because I've known you for twenty years. It's hard to take anyone seriously when you've known them that long. Especially you.

RICHIE. What do you mean by that?

PAUL. Last year it was when you saw a young couple with a child. "Oh, my God, I'll never have children." The year before it was, "Oh, my God, I'll never get that promotion." The year before that...I forget.

RICHIE. I was in the...

PAUL. Right. The hospital. Bad time. But wasn't I supportive of you on that one?

RICHIE. No.

PAUL. You're right. I didn't take that seriously, either.

RICHIE. Why?

PAUL. Richie, I have friends with cancer, AIDS, heart problems. You had a circumcision.

RICHIE. You don't think that was traumatic? I'm having a piece of my dick cut off and you bring me a book on great transsexuals in history. You are such an insensitive clod.

PAUL. Probably a lot more sensitive than your little friend was after, you know...*(makes scissoring motion with his fingers).*

RICHIE. Jesus, you are such an ass-hole.

PAUL. Excuse me, I think you're taking this a little too far.

RICHIE. I'm just stating the consensus of opinion.

PAUL. You're saying...

RICHIE. Everybody agrees.

PAUL. That...

RICHIE. You're an ass-hole.

PAUL. Because?

RICHIE. *(sings ala "Oz")* ...because of all the wonderful things he does.

PAUL. Liar.

RICHIE. Ask your friends.

PAUL. What friends?

RICHIE. Exactly.

PAUL. Good point. What the hell are you laughing about?

RICHIE. I'm not laughing.

PAUL. You are.

RICHIE. Just a little.

PAUL. You think this is fun. I nearly reach middle-age only to find out my best, my only friend, is a whining, self-absorbed, narcissist. What do you think that does to my self-esteem knowing you're it?

RICHIE. Then you acknowledge you've nearly reached middle-age?

PAUL. That's what you got out of my tirade?

RICHIE. And if we are the same age...

PAUL. I'm younger.

RICHIE. ...approximately, with a difference of a month...

PAUL. Six weeks.

RICHIE. ...if you are approaching middle-age then I certainly am approaching middle-age and my concerns regarding diminished capacity are valid.

PAUL. Your concerns about diminished capacity are possibly valid. Who knows if these concerns have any basis in fact?

RICHIE. *(quietly)* I know.

PAUL. What? I didn't hear...

RICHIE. *(quietly, emphatically)* I said I know.

PAUL. How do you...? *(beat)* Ah. I see. Diminished...

(**PAUL** *holds out his index finger, then slowly curls it to his fist.*)

RICHIE. Why don't you just yell it across the room?

PAUL. Because of the circum...

RICHIE. Has nothing to do with it. *(shrugs, embarrassed)* It just started.

PAUL. That's what this is all about? This is a Viagra story?

RICHIE. *(looking around to see who heard)* Shhh. Quiet.

PAUL. Oh, come on. Stiffen up, old man. *(beat)* Oh, I'm sorry. Poor choice of...

RICHIE. Jokes? I'm going to get jokes from you?

PAUL. *(insincerely)* You're right. I apologize. Sorry.

(**PAUL** *starts to giggle, covers his mouth.*)

RICHIE. I suppose you never had – you know.

PAUL. Never.

RICHIE. You're a lucky man.

PAUL. Nothing lucky about it.

RICHIE. Never, ever?

PAUL. Well, I lied. I did. Briefly. Sandy and I were having problems last year. A lot of anger. On both sides.

RICHIE. You never told me.

PAUL. I hinted, but you didn't pick it up. Besides, it was personal.

RICHIE. I tell you personal stuff.

PAUL. I don't. Next.

RICHIE. No, no. I want to hear. What was the problem?

PAUL. I already told you.

RICHIE. No, more specific. You know, about...

(RICHIE *does the bit with the forefinger.*)

PAUL. You want the details, you voyeuristic shit-head? You want me to embarrass Sandy by telling you about our marriage, our sex life? Is that what you want?

RICHIE. Yes. That's what I want. I want it because of your jokes, your sarcasm, your reading the fucking paper when I'm trying to tell you about me, that's what I want. I want to know what's really going on behind that smug superior expression. Yes, that's what I want.

PAUL. You want to feel good at my expense.

RICHIE. Exactly. Exactly. Just like you've been doing with me all these years.

PAUL. Not true. I've just taken what you gave me.

RICHIE. What?

PAUL. You treat yourself like shit, put yourself down, constantly crab all the time about what a shit life you have. I just went along.

RICHIE. Why didn't you ever tell me?

PAUL. I was having too much fun.

RICHIE. Exactly. And now it's my turn. So let's discuss this Viagra problem you have.

PAUL. No way.

RICHIE. With you it's a one way street.

PAUL. No, it's not. You talk seriously to me, I make jokes back at you. Back and forth, just like a real conversation.

RICHIE. Somehow, I don't find this very rewarding.

PAUL. Want a divorce from me?

RICHIE. Maybe.

PAUL. Really? Who else is going to put up with you and your whining. And then there's all this coffee and sugar I've had to consume on Sundays to keep you happy. I usually can't fall asleep 'til Tuesday.

RICHIE. Tell me, Paul, or I tell my lawyer to file the papers.

PAUL. Richie, I'm your lawyer. Anyway, I think it would be a shame now that we can engage in combat as equals.

RICHIE. *(disarmed)* Really? You think I've improved?

PAUL. Oh, yeah. You had me a little nervous there. I mean, "my Viagra problem." Very good. Had me backpedaling. *(beat)* Can I go back to my newspaper now?

RICHIE. *(preoccupied, then smiles)* Huh? Oh, sure, Paul, go ahead.

(**PAUL** *returns to reading his paper, then stops.*)

PAUL. In case I forget, happy birthday, Richie.

RICHIE. *(smug)* Oh, my happy birthday has just started. And it's going to get better. *(beat)* I mean, it was a reeeeally nice present you just gave me, Paul.

PAUL. I did?

RICHIE. The best. After all these years, you gave me a way into your soul.

(**RICHIE** *pulls his chair closer to* **PAUL.**)

So, Paul, tell me about your "Viagra problem."

THE END

PROPERTY

2 cups
Newspaper

I FEEL SWELL

I FEEL SWELL premiered at Avery Point Playhouse, 1999, directed by James Alexander Bond. It was presented at The Producers Club, 2000, again directed by James Alexander Bond, and the Midtown International Theatre Festival, 2000, directed by Charles Armesto.

CAST

CLYDE

GRETEL

HANSEL

THELMA

SETTING: Two tables, four chairs.

AT LIGHTS: **CLYDE**, **GRETEL** *and* **HANSEL** *fitfully asleep. One lies on the floor, another stretched across two chairs, the third across a table. After a pause for us to view the bodies,* **THELMA** *enters, wired and raring to go. She heads for a table.*

THELMA. *(think parakeet on speed)* Is this seat taken?

(This is addressed to the sleeping occupant at the table, **CLYDE**, *who mumbles something, but doesn't move.)*

CLYDE. Fraznitz clunkner.

(Throughout the following, none of the sleepers move.)

THELMA. Oh, good. *(sits)* I am exhausted. I just walked up from Wall Street. Eighty blocks. Figuring twenty blocks to the mile, that's about four miles. Walk, walk, walk. Nice pace, too, I'll tell you. Last couple of blocks I ran. Quick, quick, quick. I'm from Albany myself, but this is a beautiful city you have here, beautiful, but I'll tell you, it's the coffee bars I just love. Looove to death. Yes sireee, Bob. Looove to death. And they are every-where and I stopped in every one. You bet your binky I did. Eighty blocks, eighty coffee bars, eighty lattés. Whooo. Stuff reeeally keeps you on your toes and keeps you hop, hop, hopping. I'm planning to making it to Albany by dinner. What time is it now? *(looks at watch)* Three p.m. No problem. I'll just pick up the pace. Albany it is. One problem, though, one little old problem. Those lattés really whack your bladder. Take a jolt, five minutes later, BAM, it is tinkle time. *(pokes* **CLYDE** *in the ribs)* More like a gusher, I'll tell you. Ha! Listen, I gotta go gush. I'll just leave my stuff here. Could you be a sweetie and keep your eye on it? I'll be right back.

(**THELMA** *rushes out. Count five seconds and she rushes back to the table, coffee in hand. Until this point, no one has budged an inch.*)

THELMA (CONT'D) I'm baaack. Did you miss me? I gushed and got me a nice, big, creamy, oozy, doozy latté, whatte. Mmmmm, smell that aroma. Haven't had one of these in, oh, five minutes. Well, down the hatch.

(*As* **THELMA** *begins to drink,* **CLYDE**, **GRETEL** *and* **HANSEL** *begin to stir. They raise their noses in the air and sniff, like dogs on the scent. They begin moving, scratching themselves, rubbing their eyes, running their sleeves across runny noses. We see how dishevelled they are; down and outers. These are addicts and they smell a fix. Like predators, they all begin to eye* **THELMA** *and her magic latté.* **THELMA** *hasn't a clue. As she prattles on,* **GRETEL** *and* **HANSEL** *begin to circle and move in on* **CLYDE** *and* **THELMA***'s table.* **CLYDE** *tries to fight them off, jackals after the same piece of meat.*)

THELMA (CONT'D) Mmmm, mmmm, mm. Good, good, good. I could have a dozen of these. Ohh, what am I saying. I have had a dozen of these. Shit, I've had six dozen. I am such a bad girl, but I feel great. (*Sings, from "Everything's Coming Up Roses" ala Ethel Merman*) "I feel swell, I feel great, goin' to have the whole world on a plate, startin' here, startin' now, everything's coming up lattés." Ha! (*takes one long drink*) Well, this one's dead.

(**THELMA** *throws the cup on the floor and the three jackals are on it in a flash, pushing and shoving as* **THELMA**, *oblivious, sits and ponders.* **CLYDE** *wins by the time* **THELMA** *makes up her mind.*)

THELMA (CONT'D) You know, I have an urge for something. I'm not really sure what it could be. A new pair of shoes? No, that's not it. Ah, a polo mallet. No. (*brightens*) A latté. That's it. (*to* **CLYDE** *who has by now won the cup and is licking the inside*) I'll be right back. Don't go away. (*exits singing*) "I feel swell, I feel great."

GRETEL. You coulda shared.

HANSEL. You're a pig, Clyde. You see how strung out Gretel and me are. You coulda shared.

CLYDE. *(sarcastic)* Stop, you're breakin' my heart. *(pointing off-stage)* She's the pig. The fuckin' cup was bone dry. Right down to the bottom. Two drops, maybe. She must have a tongue like a lizard.

GRETEL. Hansel, if I don't get a fix soon, I'm going to do something desperate.

HANSEL. Be cool, Gretel, be cool. It ain't worth it. Don't even think what you're thinkin'. You know it never works.

CLYDE. De-cafe?

HANSEL. Ice-tea.

CLYDE. *(doubling over with nausea)* Oh, oh, that's terrible. I was really scrounging once and picked some tea shit out of the garbage, but some nitwit had put mint in it. You wanna talk disgusting. Tasted like I was drinking a shrub.

GRETEL. You gotta share the next one, Clyde. *(starts to shake)* Look. Tremors.

CLYDE. Headache?

GRETEL. *(grabs her head)* Pounding.

CLYDE. Itching?

GRETEL. *(scratches)* Madness.

CLYDE. Turtles?

GRETEL. *(grabs her stomach)* The worst. *(puzzled)* Wait. What?

CLYDE. Just to see if you were lying and I caught ya. Bullshit artist.

GRETEL. No, no, really. I need it bad, Clyde.

CLYDE. Really? *(suggestively)* Just how bad, Gretel, baby?

HANSEL. Hey, wait a second. Hold on here. This is going too far.

CLYDE. Not far enough, Hansel old pal, old buddy, old friend *(to* **GRETEL***)* What do you say, Gretel, old gal. Just how bad do you need it?

GRETEL. I've never done anything like this before, Clyde. Have a heart, man.

CLYDE. You've never had to. You're new to this kind of life, right? You used to be a "de-caffer," but now you're hooked, all right. Hooked right up to your pulse, pounding hairline. I'll ask ya again, Gretel. Just how bad do ya need it?

(HANSEL *dramatically rushes to place himself between* CLYDE *and* GRETEL.)

HANSEL. That's enough. Clyde, I'm warning you.

GRETEL. *(in a rage)* Shut the fuck up, Hansel, you Dutch deadbeat. If you hadn't blown all our money on espressos and frapachinos we wouldn't be in this fix.

CLYDE. Speaking of fix...

(CLYDE *holds out his hand for* GRETEL *who is about to go off with* CLYDE *when* THELMA *enters carrying a latté the size of a Buick. The three addicts go through paroxysms of glee, nearly fainting from the antici-pated pleasure of diving into the latté.* CLYDE *fends off* GRETEL *and* HANSEL *and helps* THELMA *to her seat.* THELMA *immediately buries her face into the huge con-tainer and stays buried for a considerable length of time. The longer* THELMA *drinks, the more the joy and vigor of the three addicts noticeably wanes until they obvious sink into despair. This scene might take a full minute.*

THELMA *finally finishes, raises her head from the con-tainer and licks her lips. She gives a YELP of joy, jumps up, runs rapidly two or three times around the stage [possibly runs into the audience then back on the stage] while the addicts follow her movements in stunned awe. She returns to her table, sits.)*

THELMA. *(with a beatific smile, she loudly sings ala Merman)* I feel swell, I feel great, I...

(She belches, then keels over and dies, face down on the table. The cup falls to the floor in front of the table.

The addicts wait, possibly five beats, then make a mad dash for the cup. Lights out.)

THE END

PROPERTY

Cup, normal size
Cup the size of a Buick (or any midsize car)

COSTUME

3 of the 4 cast are bedraggled, as if they've been sleeping in the street for years.
Dress accordingly.
Woman's coat
Woman's handbag